MW01673567

Jackie in Jacksonville

Chastity Veldt

Jackie in Jacksonville

Stand Up, Lie Down Collection

4 Horsemen
Publications, Inc.

Jackie in Jacksonville
Stand up, Lie Down

4 Horsemen Publications, Inc.

4 Horsemen Publications, Inc.
1497 Main St. Suite 169
Dunedin, FL 34698
4horsemenpublications.com
info@4horsemenpublications.com

Cover by Valerie Willis
Typesetting by Autumn Skye
Edited by V. Willis

Library of Congress Control Number: 2022930567

Paperback ISBN-13: 978-1-64450-487-1
Audiobook ISBN-13: 978-1-64450-485-7
Ebook ISBN-13: 978-1-64450-486-4

CHAPTER 1

Hello, Mankato South Grizzlies, Class of 2011! Can you believe it's been ten years? We're excited to see you again for the upcoming reunion at the Eagle Lake Yacht Club. Dinner is at 6:30 PM, drinks and dancing in the ballroom at 9:00 PM, and the memories will flow all night! Hope you can make it, fellow Grizzlies! Rawr, rawr!

Jake glared at the heavy cardstock invitation once more and sighed as he checked himself in the mirror. *Buttons straight? Yep. Shirt tucked? Also yep. Wallet? Yep yep yep.*

He pulled on his jacket, grabbed his keys and the invitation. Walking out of the hotel,he couldn't remember what kind of car he had rented, so he took a few minutes to scan the lot before finally hitting the panic button. The alarm sounded off, and he found the car. He pulled out of the parking lot and headed toward his destination. Jake was not particularly looking forward to his reunion, but he was going because his parents had begged him to go.

He called home at least once a week, but he hadn't been back to Mankato since he left on his trip nearly eight months ago, making his first stop in Milwaukee, Wisconsin.[1] That's because Jake had been touring the Midwest and Southeast as a standup comic, working as the headliner in small venues and the middle in others. Jake had just finished a conference

---

1 See *Stand Up, Lie Down #1: Molly in Milwaukee.* Now available on Kindle!

at Abraxus Tasker College[2], and flew back home for the reunion. He planned to drive to Jacksonville, leave his truck at the airport, then fly home. When it was all over, he would return to Florida and do his show in Jacksonville that week.

"It'll be good to see you, Jakey," his mom had said as he drove to the airport. "We haven't seen you in months."

"It'll be good to see you and Dad, too. I've been a little homesick."

"You'll have to get a hotel room though," she said.

"What, really?" Jake asked. "What's wrong with my old room?"

"Well, your father and I have turned it into our meditation and yoga studio. We cleaned everything out, replaced the carpet with bamboo flooring and tatami mats, and now we sit in there and meditate or do yoga. It's

---

[2] See *Stand Up, Lie Down #7: Carrie on Campus.* Now available on Kindle!

very sensual."

"Mom—" Jake squirmed in his seat, uncomfortable at the direction this conversation had taken.

"Or is that sensuous? Whichever one means sexy."

"Mom, I don't like where this conversation is go—" Jake looked for a cliff he could drive over, but he was in Florida driving to the Jacksonville airport.

"Sometimes, we'll turn on a portable heater and do hot yoga."

"Mom, please."

"Ooh, and sometimes, on a special occasion, your father will want to do hot nude yoga, which always ends up with us—"

"MOM! Okay, I'll get a hotel room."

"Thank you, dear. I don't think you'd want to sleep in there with the state it's in."

"I don't think I want to sleep in there ever again."

At the mention of yoga, Jake's mind briefly flitted back to a torrid love affair he'd had with

Betty and Sheila in Birmingham, Alabama.[3] Betty was a rich Southern belle and Sheila was her yoga instructor. His cock began to swell as he thought of the three-day threesome they'd had and their passionate declarations of love.

Then his thoughts shifted... At the mention of hot nude yoga, Jake accidentally thought of his parents doing what he and Betty had done, and his hard-on quickly vanished. And his cock hammered on his pelvic bone, begging to please be let back inside, *pretty please.*

His parents had always been rather open and frank about their personal lives, which drove Jake and his siblings crazy. "Seriously, Mom, you don't need to keep me apprised of your personal life. I only need to know that you and Dad love each other and that you remember each other's birthdays."

"Speaking of birthdays, did I tell you about

---

3 See *Stand Up, Lie Down #6: Betty In Birmingham.* The last few pages are my favorite in the entire series. — C.V.

the yoga session your father and I had on my last birthday?"

Jake dropped his phone in his lap. "Shit! Shit! Hold on, Mom. Are you still there?"

"I'm still here."

"Dammit," Jake whispered.

"Anyway, about my lovely birthday yoga session."

"What, Mom? I can't hear you. I'm going into a tunnel. My... breaking... call... later."

"Jakey, you're in Florida, there are no tunnels."

"kkkkkkkk... massive forest fire... kkkkkk. .. flames all around... "

"OK, Jakey, message received. I'll see you when you get here tomorrow. Bye-bye, Sweetie."

"Bye, Mom."

Now, after spending a few days with his family and avoiding eye contact with his parents whenever the subject of yoga came up, Jake was off to his 10-year reunion of the Grizzlies of Mankato South High.

He pulled into the Eagle Lake Yacht

Club and tossed his car keys to the valet who handed him his ticket. He walked into the Club, buttoning his jacket and looking around for anyone he knew. The foyer was empty, but there were several dozen people in the dining room off to the right. The large room was decorated in Mankato South's colors, purple and cream, with the large purple grizzly bear statue the school was known for.

Jake recalled the time that the football team from Mankato North stole their purple grizzly before the city championships. He and some of his swim team buddies stole it back before the game started as well as stealing the school's state baseball trophy and drinking celebratory beers from it after the game. Mankato South had lost 21 – 20, so they consoled themselves by getting drunk out of the stolen trophy before returning it a week later.

This grizzly looked newer than the one they had ten years ago, and Jake wondered if the old one had been stolen again but never found.

He approached the registration table and

said, "Hi, I'm here for the reunion."

"Jake Nellson?" asked the woman standing behind the table. She was slender and wore a black cocktail dress and a pearl necklace. Her hair reached down to her chin and curved around her face like a couple of parentheses. She looked like she fit right in at the Eagle Lake Yacht Club, and he recognized her as one of the "Mankato Elite" that he went to high school with.

"Nilsen," said Jake. "Is that Hatty Cooper?

"Hattie Kuper, actually," said Hattie, a touch of frost in her voice. "Kuper-Rasmussen."

"Sorry, I'll bet you get that a lot," said Jake.

"You have no idea," said Hattie.

"I can imagine. Sorry about that. It's been a while, and I've been away."

"So I hear. You're a big-time comic now, right?"

"Well, I wouldn't say big-time. How about you?"

"I'm married to Tad Rasmussen, and we have two wonderful children, Liam and Oliver.

Tad is in real estate development and I lead the local group chapter and take my boys to soccer and dance lessons. Do you want to see some pictures?"

Jake flinched. He had always thought Hattie Kuper was insufferable in high school, and he was already reaching his limit with her now. "Ohhh, maybe in a little bit."

"Great, well most everyone is here for dinner, we're just waiting for a few stragglers. You can go in and grab a seat, and we'll get started soon."

"Thank you, Hattie. It's good to see you." Jake walked away and pinned his name tag to his lapel.

Jake wandered inside and looked around. There were over a hundred men and women in the room, nearly all of them white, which you would expect in rural Minnesota. He looked for someone he knew, but despite it only being ten years since they had all been together, Jake was having a hard time recognizing most of these people.

He began to wonder if he'd made a mistake

and should just leave before anyone noticed him when he heard a voice call his name. He looked over and saw a guy stand up from a table and wave.

"Jake! Jake Nilsen! Over here!" shouted the guy.

"No, Jake Nilsen over here," Jake shouted back, pointing at himself.

"Come here, dumbass," called the guy.

Jake strode over, a grin splitting his face. "Leadweight Larsen," he said and embraced his friend in a bear hug. "How the hell are you?"

"Doing great now, buddy. Now the party can start." Ken "Leadweight" Larsen turned to a blonde woman standing next to him. "Babe, this is my buddy, Jake Nilsen. We were on the swim team together."

"Nilsen?" asked the woman.

"Er, yes?" said Jake, a bit surprised. No one ever said his name right the first time.

"Hi, I'm Alice Larson-Larsen," said Alice Larson-Larsen. She held out her hand, and Jake shook it. Alice was short, around 5'4", a true Minnesota blond with blue eyes and cannonball shoulders but a slender body like a runner's.

"Are you a swimmer too?" asked Jake.

"Triathlons, actually," said Alice. "I was a swimmer at University of Wisconsin, and I took up triathlons after I graduated."

"Badgers, eh? How'd you end up in Gopher territory?"

"That's where we met," said Ken. "I was swimming for Wisconsin and she was on the women's team."

"I thought you went to Minnesota, but I know you left," said Jake. "I never heard from you when you came back." Several of his swimming teammates all went to the University of Minnesota, although Jake was the only one good enough to make the school swim team. He was nearly on the 2016 Olympic team but missed it by a fraction of a second; he didn't like to talk about it.

"Actually, I didn't go back. I dropped out for a year and moved to Madison to work for my uncle at his company. I met the residency requirement and enrolled at UW and got on the swim team there. And that's where I met Alice. We got married a few years ago."

"And Larson-Larsen?" asked Jake.

"My maiden name is Larson, so I hyphenated."

"Ah." Jake leaned in a bit. "Do you ever get people who say your name wrong? Like, not terribly wrong, but just a tiny bit wrong?"

"Like the difference between Larson and Larsen?" asked Alice.

"Yes! Or like Nilsen and Nilssen. Or Nielsen. Or Nilsin."

"All the time! It's like people can't even hear the difference, which is weird. It's so obvious!"

"I know!" said Jake. "It's like I'm speaking a foreign language to them."

"Jeez, tell me about it," said Ken Larsen. "I don't know how many times people have asked me whether my Larsen or her Larson is first in her hyphenated name. I mean, it's pretty obvious, isn't it? It's mine, right, babe?"

"What? No! Are you kidding me right now? It's my name. Larson!"

Ken threw his head back and laughed. "Gotcha!"

Alice laughed and swatted him with her napkin. "Ass."

Jake felt a hand snake around his waist, and he turned around. "Rachel Hagen!" he exclaimed when he saw who was attached to the hand.

She squealed with excitement and leaped into his arms as he picked her up in a huge embrace. Rachel planted a big smooch on his lips and said, "Welcome home, big boy!"

Rachel was a few inches taller than Alice, a few pounds heavier, had dark brown curly hair in an upsweep hairdo that made her look like a 1940s film star. She wore a black satin dress that was cut low in the front, pushing her ample breasts together and showing cleavage so deep that, if a small child fell into it, it would prompt a national news story as rescuers tried to dig her out. Jake couldn't tell if they were natural or medically assisted, but he didn't care. They were spectacular. Her arterial-blood-spray-red lipstick shone in the lights, a little smeared after kissing Jake.

In high school, Rachel had been what your grandparents would have called "bawdy" and "brassy," or even "coarse" if your grandparents were uptight little prudes like they were in Mankato, Minnesota. She laughed loud, was raucous, loved to laugh, made inappropriate jokes, and everyone knew when she was in the room.

"You look amazing," Jake said. "Wow, I mean look at you. You look really wonderful."

"So do you," said Rachel. "The years have been most kind." She squeezed his biceps and let her eyes wander up and down his trim, muscular form a couple of times.

Jake turned and put his arm around Rachel's shoulders as he held onto her hand and pulled it around his waist. "Ken, do you remember Rachel Hagen?"

"Of course," said Ken. "You were one of

the theater kids. I remember you and Jake were in The Drowsy Chaperone with Jake our senior year. You were Janet van de Graaff and Jake was—"

"I am... Adolpho!" Jake declared, recalling his memorable line from the play. Rachel squealed and clapped her hands together, jumping up and down a little, which made her breasts jiggle.

"Hi. I'm Alice Larson-Larsen," said Alice, moving possessively closer to her husband and holding out her hand.

"Larsen-Larson?" said Rachel.

Alice rolled her eyes. "No, Lars—"

"I'm just kidding," said Rachel, winking. She shook Alice's hand and winced a little at the strength of Alice's grip. "With a name like Hagen, I get it all the time. Haugen, Hawgen, Haggen. I even convinced one guy my father was Mr. Häagen of the Häagen-Dasz ice cream company."

"What happened?" asked Alice.

"The dumbass ghosted me because he had

Type 2 diabetes and didn't want to be tempted."

"So who are you here with," asked Jake.

"Nobody, how about you?" asked Rachel.

"Same as you."

"Fine, then you're my date tonight. Is that alright?" declared Rachel; Alice visibly relaxed but didn't release her grip on Ken's bicep.

"It's the only thing keeping me here," said Jake, smiling bigger than he had all week.

During their senior year, Jake had harbored a secret crush on Rachel Hagen and had tried out for a play his sophomore year so that he could be near her. Even though Jake was one of the best swimmers in the state and fit in with the jock clique fairly well, they never quite accepted him because he was also a regular member of the theater department, appearing in any plays that didn't conflict with the swimming season or practice. He even started attending theater workshops and camps in the summer. But he never quite fit in with the theater kids either because he was a jock.

Jake never acted on his crush on Rachel,

considering her out of his league. So he just gazed at her from afar until it was time to go to college. Jake went off to the University of Minnesota, Rachel went to Hamline University, and the two lost touch.

The four of them sat at their table and chattering happily about what they had been doing since they left high school. Ken and Alice lived in Milwaukee and worked for tech startup companies. Rachel was an account manager at a marketing agency in Minneapolis. And Jake had his stand-up comedy. He didn't discuss his real estate investment or recent investment in two high-end car washes in Miami or the strip mall in Savannah, Georgia, preferring to keep his small-but-growing fortune secret.

After dinner, the four moved to the ballroom for drinking and dancing, and despite several requests from other men and women, Rachel and Jake didn't share their dancing with anyone else. They sat in a corner on a couch and talked all night, pausing only to greet old classmates who stopped by. As the night wore on and the crowd thinned out, Ken and Alice said their goodbyes and headed out the door after promising to meet for dinner the next evening.

"We should probably get out of here too," said Jake, "otherwise they'll put us on the cleanup committee."

"Ooh, they totally will. Hattie Kuper already asked me if I wanted to help out when I got here. She said my marketing experience 'would be so helpful.' Bitch. And that's after she tried to get me to look at pictures of her damn kids," said Rachel. "I said I had plans afterward and couldn't stick around. God, she was always a stuck-up bitch in high school."

"Do you have plans after this?" asked Jake.

Rachel smiled. "I don't know. Are you staying at your parents' this weekend?"

"No, I'm at the Squire Arms downtown."

"Then, no, I don't have any plans. I hear the Squire Arms has very nice rooms. Is that right?"

"Well, my room is pretty nice. I upgraded to a suite and it's pretty elegant for Mankato."

"Oh, really? That's very nice. Maybe you

could send me some cell phone photos of it," Rachel deadpanned.

"I mean, sure, but I figured you might want to come up and see for yourself."

Rachel swung her leg over Jake's lap and straddled him, her cocktail-length skirt covering her ass as she ground her crotch on his hardening cock and her cleavage pressed against his chin.

"I thought you'd never ask, Loverboy." She rubbed her pussy against his cock, and he could swear she wasn't wearing any panties.

"Oh, look at the time. We'd better go." Jake stood up suddenly, holding onto Rachel so she didn't fall backward before setting her down. Jake adjusted himself so his boner wouldn't show and hustled toward the parking lot.

"Are you two free to help with cleanup?" Hattie Kuper called after them.

"No, we have to leave urgently," said Jake.

"Sorry, Hatty Cooper," called Rachel.

"It's Hattie Kuper, goddammit," Hattie grumbled to herself. "Hattie Kuper-Rasmussen."

CHAPTER 2

"Wow, this *is* a nice suite," said Rachel, flipping on the lights. She ran over to Jake's bed and flung herself through the air and bounced when she landed on it. "Now, where were we?"

"Well, at the Yacht Club, you were straddling my lap on the couch," Jake said, gesturing to the couch several feet away.

"That's as good of a starting point as any," Rachel rolled off the bed taking Jake's hand, and guided him over to the couch. She pushed him down and straddled him once more. She kissed him deeply, grinding her pussy on his hard cock. Jake wrapped his arms around her waist and pulled her tightly to him. Rachel's breathing quickened as she continued to rock her hips and her sensitive nether regions responded to the friction.

Jake felt around on Rachel's back until his thick, strong fingers finally found the zipper, and he slowly pulled it down, opening it until he reached the end. Rachel raised up and slipped her arms out, then pulled it over her head. She was wearing a red lacy bra, and as Jake discovered, a matching red thong.

The bra looked like it was in need of a break as well as it had spent the entire night squeezing Rachel's bocce ball-sized breasts together.

"Do you like 'em? They were a gift to myself after I divorced my husband, Owen."

Jake showed his admiration for them by burying his face between them, kissing and licking Rachel's chest.

"Mmph mmm hmph hmm?" said Jake.

"What?"

Jake raised his head from the place where he hoped to die one day. "Why did you divorce him?"

"He was sleeping with my assistant."

"Ouch," said Jake. "That sucks."

"Tell me about it," said Rachel. "I haven't been able to find an assistant as good as Gary."

"Ah," said Jake. "Enough talking, more sexing."

Rachel laughed and shoved Jake's head back into her cleavage. "Agreed. Suck my big titties, Loverboy."

As Jake eagerly complied, Rachel fumbled with the buttons of his shirt, getting a few of them unbuttoned before she couldn't reach anymore. With his help and a few interruptions of his eager ministrations, she pulled his shirt over his head and gave a little gasp as she saw his rippling abs and huge pectorals.

"Oh my," she murmured. "If I had a dick, I would fuck those pecs."

"I know the feeling," said Jake, kneading her breasts with his powerful fingers.

"Oh, trust me, You're going to put your big cock between my tits. Stand up and let me see what I have to work with." She knelt and undid his belt and pants. "I hope it's not true that swimmers all have little—holy fuck, no it's not!"

As Rachel pulled down Jake's pants and underwear, his eight-and-a-half-inch prick sprang up and pointed itself at Rachel's face. "Oh my, no wonder you were popular with the girls in high school."

"Actually, I wasn't," said Jake. "I only ever wanted one girl in high school."

"Oh yeah? What happened to her?"

"Well, I'm hoping she's about to put my cock in her mouth and make a 13-year fantasy come true."

"Ewww, gross," Rachel said.

"Thirteen. YEAR. Fantasy! Not a 13-year-old's fantasy! C'mon, man!"

Rachel smiled and opened her mouth obligingly. Jake groaned as he watched his dick slip between her still-deep red lips. Rachel delicately held his shaft between a thumb and forefinger as she slowly fed herself, her mouth conforming itself to his cock as it slid, inch-by-inch, into her mouth.

Jake was mesmerized as he watched his dick nearly disappear, only two inches showing before she moved her head back and removed it from her warm mouth. When the tip of his cock reappeared, she looked up at him, smiled, and then repeated the process. She locked eyes with him as she once more returned his cock inside her mouth; Jake felt her relax her throat muscles and slide his member down her throat, her nose touching his pubic region, which he kept shaved smooth.

"Ahhhhhhh," Jake groaned as he heard all the little pops and squishes of her sucking action.

Rachel hummed her appreciation of his prick, and Jake felt the vibrations.

He nearly came right then when she did it. He thought about baseball as much as he could to hold off from jetting in her mouth.

Rachel withdrew it again, strings of thick saliva connecting her lips to his shaft, and she breathed deeply. She smiled, wrapped her long fingers around his cock, and jacked him slowly, using her honey-like saliva as lubrication, making his cock slippery. Jake could not have dreamed anything better than right now: His high school crush sucking his thick cock, taking it into her throat, and jacking him off, cupping his balls with her other hand.

As she felt his balls tighten, she stopped and said, "Not yet, I still have something I want your cum for." Rachel pronounced it "cum," instead of the right way. Jake thought, *Well, what do you expect from theatre girls?*

"That was so fucking hot," Jake said. "I love seeing you suck my cock. Your mouth is so hot and wet."

"Do you know what else is hot and wet?" she asked.

"I don't know, but I bet I'd love to taste it," said Jake.

"I'd love for you to taste it."

Rachel stood up and smiled, removing her tiny red thong. She glided over to the bed, lay back on it, and put her feet up on the bed, spreading her thighs as she did so. She exposed her nearly clean-shaven pussy, running her fingers through the closely-trimmed triangle shape cut into her pubic hair.

Jake knelt before her and lapped at her folds and the dew already emerging. He flicked his tongue on her clit and slid one of his thick fingers into her slit, noting the unintentional rhyme.

"Ooooohhh," moaned Rachel. "Yeah, baby, eat my pussy."

Jake eagerly complied, putting his mouth over her swollen labia and sucking her meaty lips into his mouth. He reached up and rubbed her clit with his thumb.

There was almost nothing Jake loved more about a woman's body than her pussy lips, swollen and red, and he loved nibbling and lightly sucking them, driving his tongue between them. Jake tended to Rachel that way, feasting on her wet snatch, lapping up her juices as she moaned and grabbed handfuls of his hair between her slender fingers. He alternated between sliding his tongue up her slit and flickering his tongue on her pink pearl. He slid two of his fingers inside her, and that's all it took to push her over the edge.

"Oh God, Jake! That's amazing. Fuck, where did you learn to eat pussy like that! Oh, don't answer, just eat me, goddammit. Eat my pussy. OH GOD OH GOD I'M CUMMING, JAKE! OH. . . GOD. . . AHHHHHHHHHHHHHH!"

Rachel clamped her thighs around Jake's head as he continued to tongue-fuck her and rub her clit.

As the waves of her first orgasm crashed over her and subsided, Rachel released her death grip on Jake's head and pulled him up. "Oh, hold off a bit, Chief. My pussy's a little sensitive after I cum."

Jake raised his head and grinned, his face shiny with her juices. "No problem. I was hoping there was something we could do."

Rachel grinned and squeezed her tits together with her hands. "Me too."

Jake climbed onto the bed and straddled

her torso, resting his cock between her tits.

"I think you need a little lubrication first," she said, opening her mouth in invitation. Jake raised up and leaned forward, guiding his cock toward her mouth. She managed to suck in an inch or two, so Jake moved forward in a plank position, his cock directly over Rachel's head. He slid his cock into her mouth as if he were fucking her face, and she moaned in appreciation.

Jake slid his member in and out as she provided counter-suction, making it like no cunt he'd ever been inside.

"Oh fuck, that feels amazing," he groaned. "I want to do that again later." He reluctantly pulled out of her mouth and consoled himself by putting his thick shaft between her tits. Rachel squeezed them together, trapping his dick, and he slid his cock in and out of her cleavage. He went slowly, enjoying the feeling of her gorgeous tits on his cock.

"All night, the guys at the reunion kept staring at my tits," said Rachel. "Some of the women, too. But all night, I only wanted you to see them and to put your mouth on them."

"Is it everything you wanted?"

"It's amazing," she gasped. "And now I want you to cum on them. What do you say, Loverboy?"

"Let's see what we can do." Jake reached down and helped her squeeze her tits together. *OK, maybe not so much helped as squeezed and played with them even as she held them for his pleasure.* "Ohh, fuck, I've dreamed of this for years," he groaned. "I've wanted to have my cock and my hands on your tits."

"Wow, you *are* a dirty little perv," Rachel said, smiling. "That's why this is so much fun."

Jake stopped for a moment. "I need some more moisture," he said as he drove forward into her eager mouth. She opened up and accommodated his shaft, letting him fuck her mouth for several seconds. As he sat back down, he pulled a pillow with him. "Lift your head," he said. As she did so, he placed the pillow under her head. "I have an idea."

He resumed his position, placed his dick back between her tits, and drove forward far enough so that his dickhead reached her lips. She smiled at his idea and accepted his cock into her mouth, providing some suction on his head with each thrust so that her mouth popped each time he pulled it out.

Soon, Jake could feel the pressure beginning to build in his balls as he continued to thrust between her globes. Then he raised up, gripped his cock, and jerked off.

"Ahh! Ahh! Here you go, baby, this load is for you. Oh, Rachel, I've dreamed of this."

"Yes! Yes!" shrieked Rachel. "Give me your hot cum!"

"GAAAAHHHH!" Jake bellowed as a rope of white cum jetted out of his cock and splashed onto her tits.

A second burst landed on her tits and reached her neck just below her chin. The third one reached nearly as far, and the fourth and fifth ropes covered her wondrous tits like the glaze on a heavenly doughnut. Rachel propped herself up on her elbows and gave Jake's dick a few quick cleaning sucks to make sure she got every drop.

Then she used her fingers to scoop up some of Jake's cum frosting and popped it into her mouth. "Mmm, that's good cum. Next time, I'm going to want it all in my mouth."

"Just there?" Jake said, breathing heavily, his face and torso slick with sweat.

"Maybe in my pussy too."

"Wherever you want," he said. "I'll give you as much as you want."

"Excellent. Then get me a towel, let's clean up, and we can figure out how much and where."

Chapter 3

"Thank you for flying with us," said the voice over the PA, four days later. "We will be departing shortly as soon as the last of our passengers are aboard." Jake returned the safety placard to the seat pocket in front of him and settled in for the connecting flight from Atlanta to Jacksonville, laying back.

A boyfriend, thought Jake. *She has a fucking boyfriend!*

It was Wednesday morning, and Jake was sitting in Business Class on his flight back to Jacksonville, where he had left his pickup in long-term parking at the Jacksonville International Airport. He had a show in Jacksonville at the

Poppers Comedy Club that weekend.

He settled in and closed his eyes as his thoughts drifted back to the previous week. He had reunited with the girl of his dreams, had the kind of sex he had fantasized about with her for the entire weekend. He had hoped this was the start of a wonderful new relationship, only to learn that she had a boyfriend.

"When can I see you again?" Jake asked Rachel as they were eating brunch in the Squire Arms restaurant Sunday morning. Both were more than a little tired — and sore and raw and fucked out — after an all-night lovemaking session that neither of them slept for more than a couple of hours. "If you'd like, I can fly you down south to one of my shows."

"Ohh, Loverboy, I wish I could. But I have a boyfriend," Rachel said, slipping a link sausage between her lips and biting down on it, severing the tube of meat in half in a ham-fisted metaphor on the part of the author.

"What, seriously? Why didn't you say

anything?" Jake didn't actually have any qualms about sleeping with someone who was already married or had a boyfriend,[4] but he was hoping this could last beyond the weekend.

"Well, it's not serious," she said. "Plus, sleeping with you was something I've been wanting to do since high school. And I finally got to do it."

"Really? Because I had a crush on you in high school," said Jake.

"Yes, really. And I had a major crush on you in high school, too."

"Why didn't you say anything?" said Jake.

"Why didn't you?" Rachel retorted.

"I don't know, I was really shy back then, and I was afraid that if you said no, then I wouldn't be able to hang out with you anymore."

"You certainly didn't seem shy last night.

---

[4] There was Randie in *Stand Up, Lie Down #1: Molly in Milwaukee;* Mandy in *Stand Up, Lie Down #4: Natasha in Nashville;* and Betty in *Stand Up, Lie Down #6: Betty in Birmingham.* Wow, Jake is a bit of a horndog, huh?

Good God, where did you learn things like that?"

"Uhh, oh, books and Internet porn."

"Uh-huh." She leaned forward and lowered her voice. "That thing you did with your tongue is not something you learn by reading or watching." She leaned back and chomped down on the remaining half of the sausage link, completing the metaphor. "Regardless of where you learned it, I'm not complaining. I've never had that done to me before."

"Not even by what's-his-name?"

"Hoo-boy, especially not by what's-his-name. He's just some guy I latched onto. He just graduated from the U a couple years ago and works at another marketing agency in town. We started out as just fuck buddies, but I think it may get serious soon."

"Then why did you and I—"

"Because it's not serious yet."

Jake took a deep swig of his coffee and got a serious look on his face.

"Oh, come on, Loverboy. I don't have to be

back in Minneapolis until tomorrow morning, and I want some more of that good fucking. What's-his-name's got nothing on you, and I need something to remember until I can teach him better. Or until the next reunion." She kicked off her shoe and rubbed her foot on Jake's crotch. She lowered her voice again. "Do you think you can fuck me a few more times before dinner with Ken and Alice?"

"That's not until seven, so I think I can manage once or twice."

"Great, because I want you to bend me over the desk and take me from behind."

Jake forked up another bite of eggs. "We're going to need some more protein then," he said, smiling.

Jake smiled as he felt for his earbuds in his jacket pocket. He may not have had a future with her, but he finally got to live out his high school fantasy with her. Several times.

"What's so funny?" said a voice next to him. Jake's eyes popped open, and a woman was sitting next to him. She was in her mid-thirties, lightly tanned, with green eyes and straight brown hair that curled near the ends and hung past her shoulders.

"Huh? Oh, uh, I was just working out a joke in my head," Jake stammered.

"Do you often laugh at your own jokes?" asked the woman.

"Only the good ones."

This made the woman smile, and he noticed the smile reached her eyes, which showed evidence of several years of joy and laughter. He smiled in return; he never trusted people who didn't have laugh lines.

"Hi, I'm Jake," said Jake.

"I'm Jackie," said Jackie. She held her hand out, and Jake took it in his and shook it. His hand was much larger than hers, but she had a strong grip that surprised him.

"Jackie from Jacksonville?" he mused.

"Yeah, my parents loved the alliteration."

"I know what you mean. I've, uh, met several people with those kinds of names over the last several months."

"Really? How do you manage that?"

"I'm a standup comic and I've been on tour for the last several months. I've got a gig in Jacksonville this weekend. How about you?"

"Ah, so that's why you laugh at your own jokes. I'm a sculptor and potter," she said, which accounted for her strong hands and forearms.

"What are your mediums? Other than clay, that is," he said.

"Well, I like to make outdoor sculptures, so for the last few years, I've worked with steel and welded pieces together, and I've done some blacksmithing. I also like working with stone, so I've done a lot with carving limestone and shaping concrete."

As Jake studied her, he could see that she was rather muscular and in great shape. She was wearing a fitted t-shirt with very short sleeves and a scoop neck. Jackie was also wearing a long skirt and a pair of sandals. Her shoulders were round and developed, her forearms were muscled, and she had strong biceps and a flat stomach.

"I'll bet moving all that iron and stone gives you a workout."

"Oh, absolutely. I really started getting in shape when I started working with outdoor sculptures. How about you? You look pretty toned up."

"I'm a swimmer," said Jake, "and I run when I can't find a pool."

"Well, there's a Y and a few gyms with pools near my studio if you need a place. Where are you staying?"

"I'm not sure yet. The comedy clubs usually have apartments, but this one doesn't for some reason. So they sometimes spring for a hotel."

"What's the club called?" she asked.

"Poppers."

"No kidding? My studio is a few blocks from there. It's in the Five Points neighborhood, and I've walked to Poppers before."

"Are there any hotels in the area?"

"Oh, plenty. And I know there are some Airbnb apartments and lofts in the area too. I've had family visit and that's where they stayed."

"Where do you live in town?"

"I live in my studio, actually. It's an old cabinet factory that I inherited from my grandfather who owned it in the 1940s. He shut the factory down in the 1960s and just used it for storage. My dad converted it into a workshop for him and his car buddies. Then, my dad passed away in 2007 and left it to my mom and me. Now the bottom floor is my studio, and I turned the second floor into a few apartments. I live in the biggest one, and a few artist friends live in two of the others. There's a painting studio in the corner and a pottery wheel and kiln in another. Then the forge and steelwork happens behind the warehouse."

"Holy shit, that sounds amazing!" said Jake. "Man, I'd love to own an old building like that."

"Yeah, you and every other asshole real estate developer in the state. Sorry, I didn't mean to call you an asshole."

Jake laughed and said, "No offense taken. I mean, it would be cool just to have an old building like that."

"I don't know how many of them have been trying to buy my building to either tear it down or tear everything out and convert it into small one-bedroom 'boho' apartments."

"Boho?"

"Bohemian. Five Points was hipster central a few years ago, and all those people want to do tiny living but still have running water. So they want tiny apartments. Fucking Millennials."

"Aren't we Millennials?" Jake said.

"Yes, and we're the *worst!*" Jackie said dramatically, flinging her arm to her forehead.

Jake smiled at that, his own eyes crinkling at the corners.

The flight attendant gave the flight safety instructions, and Jake and Jackie talked through the entire trip. He told her about life on the road as a standup comic, and she spoke of her life as a professional artist. A life that was partly possible because she owned her home and even got rent from her tenants. She didn't charge very much, she explained, because these were also artists, and housing could get expensive around Jacksonville.

Jake learned Jackie was a world-renowned artist, though, and her sculptures had been installed around the U.S., as well as Canada, Argentina, Luxembourg, and South Korea.

"Now I'm just looking for some ways to invest my money. I don't suppose standup comics know anything about wealth management, do they?"

"Actually, my old teammate, Alan Johansen, is a wealth advisor in Birmingham, Alabama. I can put you in touch with him. He's managing my portfolio and has gotten me into a couple of good real estate investments. Uhh, not tearing anything down. I own some student housing rentals in Minneapolis, and have partial ownership in a couple of car washes in Miami and a strip mall in Savannah."

"Savannah's only a couple hours from Jacksonville."

"Maybe I should go up there. I've never even seen the place."

The two talked about investments and some of the options Jake had seen over the last few years. The conversation turned to more personal subjects, and the two turned in their seats so they were facing each other, Jackie's hand resting on Jake's.

"So are you a member of the Mile High Club?" Jackie asked.

Jake blushed and stammered. "Uh, uh, uh, what?"

"Have you ever thought about, you know, screwing a total stranger in an airplane bathroom?"

"It's a little early in the book for that, don't you think?" said Jake.

"What?"

"What? I mean, I would love to, but we're going to land in fifteen minutes, and I'd like to think I'd take a little longer than that."

"Oh, jeez!" shrieked Jackie, laughing uproariously. "I didn't mean us! Oh my God, that's so embarrassing. I was just— I'm so bad at flirting and being sexy and I just said the first thing that came to mind! And I can't believe I said any of that."

Jake laughed with her and said, "Don't feel bad. I'll tell you a secret about myself. I'm bad at dirty talk unless I'm actually in the act at that moment. Like, right now, if we were trying to talk dirty to each other, I would stammer and get all embarrassed. But if I'm actually having sex, I can talk dirty like it was my job."

There was a chime overhead, interrupting the awkwardness that both of them were feeling. The flight attendant's voice came over the PA and said, "Ladies and gentlemen, the captain has turned on the seatbelt sign which means we will be landing in a few minutes. So if you could fasten your seat belts, please."

"If we could fasten our seat belts what?" said Jackie. "What will happen? That's an incomplete sentence, dammit!"

Jake laughed. "Marry me."

Jackie laughed with him. "It depends on your view of the Oxford comma."

"It's a must. Otherwise you get, 'We invited

the strippers, JFK and Stalin,'" Jake said, quoting the old Internet meme on the subject.

Jackie squeezed his hand. "I've always wanted a June wedding. We'll keep it small, about thirty people total."

The two laughed and faced forward, but Jackie didn't release his hand, and Jake didn't pull away.

As the two were walking through the airport, hand in hand, Jackie said, "Well, this is where I leave you, Jake Nilsen. I have to go down and catch an Uber."

"Actually, I could drive you, if you'd like," Jake said. "I parked my truck here last week and I'm heading over to Poppers. Since you're close, I can give you a lift."

"I would love that. Thank you."

The two caught a shuttle to long-term parking, stowed their luggage in the back of the specially-locked truck bed, and Jake had Jackie punch her address into his GPS.

When they arrived at her building, Jake whistled admiringly. "Wow, she's a real beauty.

I can see why you want to save her from the developers. And I love the sculpture out front. I'm guessing that's one of yours."

"Yes, it was the first metal sculpture I ever did, after doing concrete and limestone for several years."

"I can understand why your stuff is installed around the world."

"Aww, thank you. That's very kind."

"Say, I have to go check-in at Poppers and let them know I'm here and find a hotel, but I don't have a show until tomorrow. I've had a great time talking with you. Could I take you to dinner tonight?"

"Sure, that would be great. And I didn't want to offer earlier, because I didn't know you very well. But if you're interested, I actually have a very small apartment that's empty right now. You can stay there for the week. I'll loan you some sheets and a towel, and you can use that while you're here. No charge!"

"That would be great," said Jake, smiling a bright smile.

"Wonderful. Let me show you where to park then you can go up and I'll give you the key. You can check-in then come back and rest before we leave."

Chapter 4

"Hi, I'm looking for Cherie. Is she around?" Jake was in the bar area of Poppers Comedy Club. A few staff members were cleaning up and getting the place ready for tonight's open mic.

"She's in the back office," said one of the servers, pointing to a hallway with a sign that said "RESTROOMS" hanging over it.

"Is she in the men's or women's?" asked Jake.

"Let me guess, you're a comic," said the woman, rolling her eyes.

"Um, no," mumbled Jake. "I sell, uh, matchbooks." He hurried down the hall, spotting a third door that said, "Manager." He knocked and the door opened.

"Can I help you?" said the woman who answered the door. She was tall and blonde, a little heavyset, and wore tan pants and a womens polo shirt.

"Are you Cherie?" asked Jake.

"Guilty," said Cherie. "Are you Jake Nilsen?"

"No, Nil—er, wait, yes. Nilsen." *This is weird. Twice in one book? That* never *happens,* thought Jake.

"I was just looking at your headshot that your manager sent over. Plus he told me how to pronounce your name right."

"Ah."

"Cookie?" Cherie offered him one from a plate of chocolate chip cookies she'd been enjoying before he knocked.

"Ooh, don't mind if I do. I love chocolate chip. Thank you very much."

"You're welcome. I made 'em myself," said Cherie. They were excellent and Jake said as much.

"So, do you need a hotel tonight? I wasn't

sure if you'd want a place. We've got an apartment, but it got annihilated a couple of weeks ago by Curtis Sanders and his girlfriend, Anna. Apparently, another friend of theirs, Debi, came to visit, and the three of them trashed the place with some marathon sex session. I got complaints from the neighbors and I'm having the place steam cleaned now. And redecorated."

"Shit, that's incredibl. . .y rude and terrible," said Jake, deciding not to admit to knowing Curtis. He and the other comic had a tradition of sharing their sex stories with each other in a competition. The loser had to buy the winner dinner, and Jake was worried this story would be a five-star meal winner. "Whoever this Curtis guy is, I hope he's ashamed of himself."

"Oh, come off it," laughed Cherie. "I know he's your friend. Sherie, the manager at Popcorn in Atlanta, is a friend of mine. She told me about the last time the two of you were in town.

Alyssa says hi, by the way."[5]

Cherie winked, and Jake's face turned red as he smiled at the memory. Alyssa was the annoying-but-sexy server at Popcorn he had spent that weekend having athletic sex with.

"So what about that hotel, stud? We can set you up with a Best Western about twelve miles from here. It's cheap, but it's clean."

"No need," said Jake. "A friend has an apartment she's going to let me borrow while I'm here. She's just a couple blocks from here." Jake described the former warehouse and its proximity to the club.

"Oh, sure, I know that place," said Cherie. "There's a really cool sculpture out front."

"That's my friend's sculpture. I'll let her know you like it."

The two chatted a little longer before Jake excused himself to go back to Jackie's apartment to shower and get ready for dinner.

---

[5] See *Stand Up, Lie Down #5: Alyssa in Atlanta.*

"Florida lobster tails for the lady, and for you, big guy?" said the server, looking at Jake expectantly, pen and pad at the ready. Jake and Jackie were at the Barnacled Hull, one of the local seafood restaurants near Jacksonville Beach. They were sitting in a booth near the open wall, looking out at the ocean and listening to the crashing of the waves.

"I'll have the mahi mahi with spicy rice," said Jake. "Thank you."

The server took their menus and left.

"Man, we don't have weather this nice in Mankato in November," Jake said, looking out at the ocean.

"Is that where you were?" asked Jackie.

"My 10-year class reunion was this weekend and my parents talked me into going."

"No kidding? My 15-year reunion is coming up next year. I don't know if I'll go." she shrugged.

"Why not?" asked Jake.

"I didn't have a great high school experience. I was one of the arty kids. People either ignored me or hassled me. I just kept to myself or hung out with a few friends. What about you? I'll bet you were real popular in high school. That blonde hair and great body. Were you on the swim team?"

"Yes, I was on the swim team, but no, I wasn't that popular. I was also in the theatre, so neither clique fully included me. I was too actor-y for the swimmers and too athletic for the actors. I hung out with both groups, but I was the tagalong."

"And how was the reunion?"

"It was. . . pretty great. I saw some old friends and got to spend some time with a few people I knew."

Jake could feel himself get a little melancholy, and he knew he would mope all night if he let the mood take hold. So he raised his beer in a toast, and Jackie raised her white wine.

"To art," he said. "May we always have beautiful things to look at."

"To comedy," said Jackie. "May we always

have corny things to laugh at."

Jake snickered. "To comedy. But I was serious."

"Aww, thank you." Jackie blushed and looked out at the ocean. The evening wind blew in and blew her hair across her face. She combed it behind her head with her fingers. The two chatted for a few more minutes until their food arrived, and they dug in. They enjoyed the food for a while, and Jackie spoke up. "So what do you do when you're not doing comedy? Do you have a regular job?"

"No, I've just been living on the road for the last several months. I drive from venue to venue, do my shows, and then move on to the next one. This week, I flew home for the reunion, and I'm doing this show, then my tour is officially over. My agent thinks she can set me up with another seven or eight shows out west, but I'm still wondering if I want to go all the way out there or just stick with the eastern half of the U.S. for another year. Or maybe I'll stay somewhere for a month and relax."

"Lots of beautiful women out west," said Jackie.

"Lots of beautiful women right here," said Jake.

Jackie smiled and looked down at her plate. "So about the wedding," she said.

Jake turned pale. "Oh! Uhh, were you...?"

Jackie threw her head back and laughed. "Jesus, Jake, you look absolutely panicked! I was kidding, you dope."

"Ohh," Jake breathed a sigh of relief. "That was a good one."

"So when do you have to decide about the next leg of your tour?"

"I probably will take a month off and then go wherever he can get me booked."

"Where will you stay in the meantime?"

"Oh, I don't know. I might go down to Miami and visit the car washes, or head up to Savannah and finally see the strip mall. Or I may just fly home and hang out there."

"Eww, Mankato in December? I can't imagine being that cold for so long."

"It's not so bad. You get used to it."

"You're not cold now?" asked Jackie. She was wearing a light sweater and rubbed her arms to warm them up.

"No, are you kidding? This is beautiful. Are you cold?"

"It's getting a bit cool," she said. The temperature was seventy-two degrees, which Jake and all of Mankato, Minnesota, considered a warm spring day.

"Why don't you slide around here then. I'll keep you warm."

Jackie smiled and slid over to Jake, who put his arm around her. She leaned into him and breathed his scent in. It was a manly, musky scent, a combination of his body and his cologne.

"I feel safe with you," she said.

She took another deep breath of him and stroked his thigh with her fingertips. Jackie gasped as she saw the outline of Jake's eight-and-a-half-inch dick swell in his pants. Jake kissed the top of her head in response.

"Did... did... I do that?" she asked, looking up at him, a hint of nervous longing in her eyes.

Jake kissed her forehead. "I'm afraid you did."

She looked at it, and her hand moved toward it then jerked away as if it were a hot stove. "Can I touch it?"

"Yes. Please," Jake whispered hoarsely.

Jacke pinched it lightly between her thumb and forefinger and poked it to see how hard it was. It was like iron now, and Jackie knew how to work with iron. She squeezed it between her fingers and the heel of her hand, running it up and down the length of his shaft.

"I'd love to see this in person," she said.

"Check, please," he called to the server.

He dropped several twenties on the table, and the two left like the server was about to ask them to be on the cleanup committee.

Chapter 5

"You'll have to be gentle with me," Jackie said in Jake's ear as he kissed and licked her neck. She wrapped her legs around his waist, and he held her up in the large service elevator in her warehouse. "I don't know if I'll be able to get all of that inside me."

She had gotten a preview as Jake had driven them back from the restaurant. She pulled out his cock and had given him a slow handjob as they drove, stopping before he came, leaving his ballsack full of come.

"We'll take it as slow as you need," he said.

He cupped one of her breasts in his hand and held her up with his other. Her breasts were smaller but perky and firm, about the size of tennis balls. Each. They were each the size of a tennis ball. Not both of them together were the size of a single tennis ball. That would be weird. Plus, where would you even put the nipples?

Jesus, would you quit that? thought Jake. *I'm trying to concentrate here.*

Sorry, said the author. *I've been drinking.*

Jake had been sneaking tiny glances at Jackie's cleavage most of the night and had been hoping he could get a good look at her tits up close. He was about to get his chance.

Jackie handed Jake her key and said, "It's the door on the left."

Jake let them in and kicked the door shut behind him. He carried her to the couch and plopped onto it with her straddling his lap. Jackie lifted her skirt to her hips, and Jake helped her take off her t-shirt and bra. He kissed and licked her breasts, enjoying their size and shape, which, as described earlier, were like tennis balls. But they weren't yellow and fuzzy, just smooth and normal skin—

Seriously! Stop it! thought Jake.

Sorry, sorry. I'm good. Won't happen again.

He gently squeezed them, sucking one of her nipples into his mouth and pinching the other, making her moan. She ran her fingers through his hair and arched her back, urging him to suck and lick her harder. Jake pulled her back up and slowly lifted her skirt; she helped him, pulling it over her head. Then she unbuttoned his shirt and slid it over his head. He pulled her against his chest and wrapped his arms around her so he could feel her bare skin against his. She licked his ear and nuzzled his neck, giving small kisses and tiny sucks in the crook of his neck.

"I love the feeling of our skin together," he said. "You're so soft and silky and I love how you feel against me."

The two kissed and licked each other's neck, just enjoying the feeling of their skin against each other. Jake was able to reach his hands around to the opposite sides of her ribs, his left hand on her left ribs and right hand on her right ribs. He ran his fingers up and down her ribs, feeling each one like he was counting them as she drove her tongue hard against his neck.

"Oh, fuck, your tongue feels wonderful," he murmured.

He shifted his hands and kneaded her strong back muscles as she stayed mashed against him, grinding her cunt against his raging hard-on, still in his pants.

"I want to see it," she said. "Let me see your dick."

They stood up, Jake standing several inches taller than her. She undid his belt and opened his pants. Jake slid them down and kicked them off, and Jackie removed her lacy purple panties. She held Jake's cock like she was shaking hands with it and stroked it in an underhanded motion.

"This *is* a big one," she said. "I hope this will fit in my pussy."

"Do you want to suck it?" he rasped.

"I'm not very good at it," she said.

Jake sat back on the couch and pushed his

hips forward. Jackie knelt in front of him and licked his head and shaft a few times before she put it in her mouth. She tried to take as much in as she could but could only manage a few inches before she had to stop.

"I'm sorry," she said. "I'm sorry, I wish I could suck more."

"Never apologize," said Jake. "I've got a beautiful woman putting my cock in her mouth. There's nothing I could ever complain about."

Jackie smiled and sucked him back in. She bobbed her head up and down, using her fist to jack him off as she sucked. Her hair fell and blocked Jake's view of the beautiful sight, so he pulled it gently back to reveal her green eyes gazing up at him as she worked his prick in and out of her mouth. He watched the suction she was putting on his dick, watched her cheeks hollow out with the pressure, and could feel his come rising. He was getting close to a release.

She would pause every so often, lick the sides of his shaft again for lubrication, then return to her sucking and pumping. Jake could feel the pressure build in his ball sack, and he squirmed in anticipation.

"I'm going to come in a minute, baby. Where do you want me to come?" he said, using the proper pronunciation of "come." He figured anyone who loved the Oxford comma would say it that way instead of "cum."

"Not yet," she said, removing his cockhead with a *pop*. "I want you to eat my pussy first."

Jake groaned in frustration. That was twice she had postponed his release. She sat down next to him on the couch and he took her place on the floor, nestled between her slender, powerful thighs. Jake pulled her hips toward him so they were on the edge of her couch. He kissed and licked his way up one thigh, sliding his tongue in the crevice where her leg and her pelvis met, and skipped over her wet cunt, licked the other crevice, then worked his way back down her other thigh.

"Oooooh, Jake. You missed my pussy. Please eat my pussy. Please," she moaned. Jackie squirmed as he further opened her thighs like he was opening a precious treasure, revealing her pink folds and swollen labia.

She rested her legs over his shoulders, her small feet resting on his V-shaped back. Jake licked the entire length of her wet cunt once, twice, three times, like he was eating an ice cream cone on a hot summer day. Jake lapped at her lips, pausing once in a while to suck her labia into his mouth. Jackie's juices flowed as he continued his tender ministrations to her wetness. Each stroke of his tongue slid over her hard clitoris, which he gently massaged with his thumb as he lapped at her lips.

"Ohhhhhh, Jake, lover, I'm going to come. You're making me come with your mouth. Ohh, you'd better stop, or I'll come in your mouth. No, Jake, ahhhhh! Jake, ahhhhhhhh! JAKE, STOP! I'M GOING TO COME IN YOUR MOUTH!"

Jake looked up and met her eyes but didn't stop licking. He smiled even as his tongue worked its magic, and he gripped her forearms with his strong hands.

"OHHH, GOD. YOU WANT THIS! YOU WANT ME TO COME IN YOUR MOUTH!" Jackie shrieked, writing in delicious agony as he continued sliding his tongue up her drenched pussy, flicking it over her hard pearl. "OH, FUCK, LOVER! I'M... OH GOD, GET READY. . . HERE I GO ... IN YOUR MOUTH ... I'M ... OHHH! OHHH! AAAAAAAAA!!!!"

Jackie bucked and writhed as her first orgasm washed over her, and still Jake continued licking her, working her back up toward her second.

"OHH, Jake, I'm going to come again. Ohhhhh, what are you. . .? That's so good. . . What are you. . .? AAAAAAAAA!!!!" And she bucked her hips again, more violently than the first one, pulling him toward her with her feet, even as Jake held onto her arms. "I'M COMING AGAIN! I'M COMING — AAAAAA!!!"

"Oh, God!" she gasped, trying to catch her breath after the waves finally subsided. "No more. No more. I need. A break. Oh, fuck."

Jake sat back, grinning, his face shiny with her wetness. "You taste amazing," he said. "I loved licking up your juices as you came."

"I'm ready for you to come now, too, lover. Fuck my wet pussy."

Jake positioned himself so his eight-and-a-half-inch cock was at her entrance. He slid his cockhead up and down between her meaty labia, getting it wet with her fluids.

"Ohh, please, Jake. I can't take it. Please put it in me. Please shove that fat cock in me as far as it'll go."

"Do I get to come this time?" he said with a smile.

"Anything you want, lover. Please fuck me with that giant cock."

Jake slid his thickness into her a couple of inches which made her gasp: "HOOOOLY FUCK!" He slid nearly all the way back out and immediately pushed back in again, going in another inch.

"OH, GOD," she said. "Give me a minute.

Just stay for a minute." Jake could feel Jackie's cunt muscles tense and relax, tense and relax, as she accommodated her lover's cock.

"Okay, do it again," she said with a nod. Jake pulled out to the same point and slowly pushed his way back into her pussy, watching her lips open to accommodate his veiny, hard rod. He made it nearly all the way in that time, so he waited again, flexing his cock and making it bounce.

"Ow, shit! What was that?" she said, laughing. "Did you bounce your dick in me?"

"Yep. Guy kegels." He bounced it again.

"Ohh, fuck. That feels weird. I love it."

Jake bounced it a couple more times then slid his cock out one more time. She could feel the emptiness where he had left her. Jake grabbed Jackie's hands and pushed one more time — "FFFFFUUUUCK!" she cried — this time driving himself into her so deeply, he was buried to the hilt in her hot cunt.

"Oh, God, you're in me. You're all the way in me," she babbled. "I feel so full. I've never had a cock this big in me. Oh, I love this cock. Fuck me, fuck me, lover. Fuck me with your big cock."

Jake was only too happy to oblige. Still gripping her hands, Jake slid out then drove himself forward, making her gasp again. He pulled out one more time and pushed in again. Out, in. Out, in.

"Ohh! Ohh! Ohh!," Jackie grunted with each thrust. "Ohh! Ohh! That's so fucking good."

Jackie's pussy grew to accept the fleshy invader and Jake was able to speed up his rhythm until he was pulling her toward him as he pushed himself into her, their bodies slapping with each powerful thrust.

"Ohh! Ohh! Ohh!" Jackie yipped. "I'M COMING AGAIN! OH, FUCK, JAKEY, I'M COMING ON YOUR BIG COCK! OHHHHHHHHHH!" Jackie thrashed and bucked as Jake grabbed her hips and continued driving himself into her eager cunt.

"I'm gonna come too, baby," he finally said. "I'm gonna come too! Where do you want my hot come."

"Come on me!" she said. "Pull out and come on me. I want to see it. You can come in me later, but now I want your hot come on my stomach."

Jake didn't need any more urging. He pulled out of her now-gaping pussy, grabbed his cock in his fist, and jacked off. He looked into Jackie's beautiful green eyes as she was breathing hard and stroking his forearms while he jerked himself to completion.

"This is for you, Jackie. I'm gonna come for you, Jackie. Oh, God, baby, take my come. UNGH! UNGH! UNGH! UNGH!"

The first thick shot of jizz shot out and left a rope several inches long, frosting Jackie's flat belly. "OH!" she gasped as she felt the hot juice hit her skin.

The second blast fired further and landed between her tits, leaving a trail longer than the first. "Oh, yessss!" hissed Jackie.

The third come rope landed almost as long as the second, on Jackie's breast and trailing down to her pubis. The fourth and fifth shots were just honored to be included, and they made a good showing, landing a few inches past Jackie's belly button.

Jackie quickly pivoted on the couch until her face was next to Jake's cock, and she sucked the remaining come out of the tip. Then she lay back as Jake sat back on his heels, both of them gasping for air.

"Oh, fuck, that's amazing," said Jake. "You look so fucking hot with my come on you."

"I feel dirty," she said. "Good dirty. This is what I wanted. I was actually fantasizing about it on the plane when we were talking. I just didn't dream it would actually happen."

"I'm certainly glad it did," said Jake, giving a little post-coital shudder. "I was thinking some of the same things."

"Oh yeah? You fantasized about coming on me?"

"On you. In you. In your mouth. Yes, I did."

"I want all of those, plus a few more variations," Jackie said, stroking Jake's arm. "In fact, if you can help me out in the shower, we can probably manage another of those."

Jake stood up and helped Jackie to her feet. She still had his come running down her torso. She scooped up some of his jizz on her finger and popped it into her mouth.

"Oh yeah, we can definitely manage those," she said, turning and walking toward her bathroom. "I know which one I want next."

"As you wish," said Jake.

"By the way," Jackie said as they stepped into the bathroom. "I don't have any plans for that apartment for a while. If you want a place to stay while you decide whether to go on your next tour, you're welcome to it."

"I may take you up on it," Jake said. He pushed the door closed behind him, leaving it open just a little bit.

Chastity Veldt

Having years of humor writing and publishing under her belt, Chastity has turned to writing humorous erotica. Puns and fourth wall breaking are only some of the entertainment Chastity Veldt will bring her readers. With a passion for fun reads and awkward moments, her debut series "Stand Up, Lie Down" will delight erotica readers with a fresh new feeling.

More Chastity Veldt Books

Molly in Milwaukee
Irene in Indianapolis
Lydia in Louisville
Natasha in Nashville
Alyssa in Atlanta
Betty in Birmingham
Carrie on Campus
Jackie in Jacksonville
Vanessa in Vancouver
Erika in El Paso

More books from 4 Horsemen Publications

Erotica

Ali Whippe
Office Hours
Tutoring Center
Athletics
Extra Credit
Financial Aid
Bound for Release
Fetish Circuit
Now You See Him
Sexual Playground
Swingers

Dalia Lance
My Home on Whore Island
Slumming It on Slut Street
Training of the Tramp
The Imperfect Perfection
Spring Break
72% Match
It Was Meant To Be... Or Whatever

Honey Cummings
Sleeping with Sasquatch
Cuddling with Chupacabra
Naked with New Jersey Devil
Laying with the Lady in Blue
Wanton Woman in White
Beating it with Bloody Mary
Beau and Professor Bestialora
The Goat's Gruff
Goldie and Her Three Beards
Pied Piper's Pipe
Princess Pea's Bed
Pinocchio and the

Blow Up Doll
Jack's Beanstalk
Pulling Rapunzel's Hair
Curses & Crushes

NOVA EMBERS
A Game of Sales
How Marketing Beats Dick
Certified Public Alpha (CPA)
On the Job Experience
My GIF is Bigger than Your GIF
Power Play
Plugging in My USB
Hunting the White Elephant
Caution: Slippery When Wet

SHAE COON
Bound in Love
Controlling Assets
For His Own Protection
Her Broken Pieces

LGBT EROTICA

DOMINIC N. ASHEN
Steel & Thunder
Storms & Sacrifice
My Three Orc Dads: a Novella

ESKAY KABBA
Hidden Love
Not So Hidden

GRAYSON ACE
How I Got Here
First Year Out of the Closet
You're Only a Top? You're Only a Bottom?
I Think I'm a Serial Swiper
Lookin in All the Wrong Places

What Makes
Me a Whore?
A Breach in
Confidentiality
Back Door Pass
My European Adventure
An Unexpected Affair
Finding True Love

LEO SPARX
Before Alexander
Claiming Alexander
Taming Alexander
Saving Alexander
The Case of Armando

CPSIA information can be obtained
at www.ICGtesting.com
Printed in the USA
LVHW011532250222
712023LV00006B/533

9 781644 504871